Python Play
and other recipes for fun

Poems by Robert Heidbreder ★ Pictures by Karen Patkau

Stoddart
Kids
TORONTO • NEW YORK

Published in Canada in 1999 by
Stoddart Kids,
a division of Stoddart Publishing Co. Limited
34 Lesmill Road
Toronto, Canada M3B 2T6
Tel (416) 445-3333 Fax (416) 445-5967
E-mail Customer.Service@ccmailgw.genpub.com

Distributed in Canada by
General Distribution Services
325 Humber College Blvd.,
Toronto, ON M9W 7C3
Tel (416) 213-1919 Fax (416) 213-1917
E-mail Customer.Service@ccmailgw.genpub.com

Published in the United States in 2000 by
Stoddart Kids,
a division of Stoddart Publishing Co. Limited
180 Varick Street, 9th Floor
New York, New York 10014
Toll free 1-800-805-1083
E-mail gdsinc@genpub.com

Distributed in the United States by
General Distribution Services
85 River Rock Drive, Suite 202
Buffalo, New York 14207
Toll free 1-800-805-1083
E-mail gdsinc@genpub.com

Canadian Cataloguing in Publication Data

Heidbreder, Robert
Python play and other recipes for fun

Poems.
ISBN 0-7737-3213-6

I. Play – Juvenile poetry.   2. Children's poetry, Canadian (English).*
I. Patkau, Karen.   II. Title.

PS8565.E42P97 1999   jC811'.54   C98-932827-9
PR9199.3.H44P97 1999

THE CANADA COUNCIL | LE CONSEIL DES ARTS
FOR THE ARTS | DU CANADA
SINCE 1957 | DEPUIS 1957

*We acknowledge for their financial support of our publishing
program the Canada Council, the Ontario Arts Council, and
the Government of Canada through the Book Publishing
Industry Development Program (BPIDP).*

Printed and bound in Hong Kong, China Book Art Inc., Toronto

for Jane
— R.H.

for Michael
— K.P.

Recipe for Play

I tire-swing the monkey bars,
leapfrog the slippy slide,
hide and seek the skipping rope,
hopscotch a wheelbarrow ride.

I throw in things I love to do,
add a mixed up name or two,
cook up a silly game-time stew
that I can eat my play-day through!

4

Mirror Mirror Me

Hello, mirror, mirror me!
In you another me I see!

I see I see a muddy shirt.
I see some jeans all caked with dirt.
I see two running shoes unlaced.
I see I see a dusty face.
I see I see one missing sock,
I see a pocket stuffed with rocks.
I see a torn and ripped-out knee.
I see in you a matching me,
Kind of scruffy, kind of muddy
So you'd be a perfect buddy.
You're the perfect match for play.
Won't you leave your mirror today?
Come on — mirror, mirror me!
Leave that mirror and be free!
Come on out and play with me!

(Originally published by Houghton-Mifflin, CANADA, in the WAVES Guidebook, 1993)

Leapfrog

Paul leaped over Tara,
And Tara over Greg.
Greg sprung over Elim,
Who bounded over Peg.

Peg hopped over Harjeet,
Who tumbled over Bill.
Bill crashed into Soo-Wing,
Who toppled down the hill.

Noam bounced over Maya,
Who vaulted over Ted.
Ted rushed into Niki,
Who pounced on little Fred.

6

Fred rolled onto Shenny.
She bounded over Ruth,
Who stumbled into Dino —
Out popped his loose front tooth!

Dino crashed on Sammy,
Sam on Caroline,
Who pirouetted lazily
In the soft sunshine.

Carol lunged at Justin,
Who faked a funny fall.
Then hurdled onto Chad,
Who simply walked on Paul.

Paul began to wobble
And rolled off like a log.
Then all the children
Cheered and yelled,
"Let's play again! LEAPFROG!"

7

Bicycle Wheels

Bicycle wheels,
    whir me around,
    whir me through streets
    all over the town,
    whir me up hills
    and into high jumps,
    through the swift air
    and over dirt bumps.

    Whir me past houses,
    through lanes, to the park,
    then whir me back home
    as the sky's turning dark.

And bicycle wheels,
    whir on in my head,
    whir me to sleep
    in my bicycle bed!

Summer Tickles Me

Up the tree trunk,
    barefoot I'll climb
    tickling the tree
    to see summertime.
Tall at the top,
    I'll stop and I'll stare,
    and let summer's leaves
    tickle my hair.
Down the tree trunk,
    I'll shimmy and slide
    singing with summer
    that tickles inside.

10

Somersaulting
the Seasons

I'll somersault,
     somersault
     through the summer days.
I'll autumn-sault,
     autumn-sault
     in the smoky haze.
I'll winter-sault,
     winter-sault
     across the snowy ground,
And spring-sault,
     spring-sault,
     as spring comes rolling 'round.

I'll somersault,
     autumn-sault,
     winter-sault and spring,
     for the tumbling changes
     the seasons bring.

11

Song
of the Tire Swing

"Pop on me,"
       the tire swing sings.
"I'll wheel you 'round in dizzy rings.
Plop on, brother,
Flop on, sister,
I'm a reeling real-live twister.
See the world go swirling by,
you'll feel you're circling in the sky.

Round and 'round you'll topsy-turve
Whizzing out a dizzy curve.
I'm sleek and slick and wheelie-quick.
Just promise me
         you won't get sick!"

A MUDDY MONSTER

sticky icky crud crud crud
ooey gooey mud mud mud
gloopy gloppy goo goo goo
mud mud mud I'll play in you!

    I'll press you and
    pat you into a pie,
    then paint on a mustache
    and blacken each eye.
    I'll glump on a beard
    that's goopy and thick,
    that's whirly and curly
    and wickedly thick!
    I'll slop on mud boots
    up to my knees
    and slap on mud hair
    wherever I please.
    Some fangs, some warts,
    a scar or two,
    Oh, mud, I'll muddy myself with you!
    And when I'm a muddy cruddy mess
    a muddy monster in muddy dress,
    I'll go for the hose,
    and stand in the spray,
    and wash my muddy buddy away.
    Then . . .
        I'll run back in the muddy fray
        and start again my muddy play!

Slide Rides

Head first,
     on my belly
Feet first,
     roll like jelly
On my back,
     like a rag
Rolled up tight,
     like a bag
In the rain,
     wet bum for trying
On wax paper,
     just like flying
Spread out wide
     or on my side
How I love to ride
       and
         glide,
            zip
              and
                whip
                   on
                     down my slide!

16

17

Parachute Play

we'll . . .
pull down and lift,
    so up floats a dome,
    run under the dome
    then run again home.

don't let it fall,
    we'll holler and hoot,
    don't you get trapped
    by the cloud parachute.

but if you get trapped,
    as down falls the dome,
    we'll yank it and lift it
    and send you on home.

18

Parachute Sail

we
pull it and shake it,
    it billows and flows —
    up foam the waves
    as silk winds blow.

set sail in the sea
    and chart out your route,
    ride through the storm
    of the wild parachute.

but if you sink down
    in the parachute sea
    we'll send out fresh sailors
    to sail you home free.

and if they get lost
    as they're searching for you,
    we'll stop making waves
    till the rescue is through.

A Helicopter Spin

MOM!   DAD!
Lift me up for a helicopter twirl!
I'll be the blades --
                    SWISH!   SWIPPITY!   SWIRL!

Grab an ankle!
            Hold a wrist!
Soar me a whirly,
                a turny twist!

While I spin,
            I'll CHOP! CHOP! CHOP!
Then land me softly,
                    PLISHITY!   PLOP!

MOM!   DAD!
Lift me up for a helicopter whir,
so I'll see the world
                    in a whirl-about blur.

21

The Fastest Runner

I leap across all hurdles.
      I sprint upon my hands.
I dash along sea beaches
      on scorching summer sands.
I shoot up icy mountains
      in grueling winter freeze.
I speed past roaring rivers
      like a cyclone in the trees.
I take on every challenge.
      I win at every race.
Oh, I'm the fastest runner,
      I'm sheer energy and grace.
Yes, I'm the fastest runner,
      all my friends and foes agree,
When my imagination
      runs away with me.

23

Best Friends

See saw teeter totter
I'm the pot
And you're the potter

Hopscotch scoot along
I'm the music
You're the song

Swinging swings low and high
I'm the earth
You're the sky

Skipping rope in and out
I'm around
You're about

Run a race fast or slow
I'm the stop
You're the go

Having fun me and you
That's the best thing
Best friends do!

25

26

Python Play

Keep your eye out for a python,
     sneaking 'round to meet you,
     peeking through the waving grass,
     sleeking up to greet you.

Keep your eye out for this python,
     its darting tongue can tease you,
     its slapping, wrapping body could
     just slip around and squeeze you.

If you spot this python,
     this and not another,
     don't yell for help,
     don't faint away,
     it's just my reptile BROTHER!
     He loves his silly python —
     he says it's so fantastic!
     And I promised not to tell
     but. . . .

     SHHHHHHHHshhhh!. . . .
     it's only plastic.

27

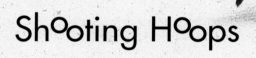

Shooting Hoops

Dribble
        dribble
                bang
                        AND! . . .
                                miss

Dribble
        dribble
                clang . . .
                        AND! . . .
                                miss

Dribble
        dribble
                whack . . .
                        AND! . . .
                                miss

Someday
        I'll
                get
                        the
                                knack
                                        of
                                                this!

28   Dribble . . . . . dribble . . . . . SCORE!

29

Skipping Out

When I'm mad,
        I just skip out.
I grab a rope
        and skip about.
I skip around
        on a skipping trip.
Backwards and forwards,
        I skip skip skip.

Up the block, across the street,
My feet keep tapping a snappy beat —
A-SNIP   A-SNAP   A-TAPPITY-TIP —
I skip at a super skipping clip.

And when I've skipped the neighborhood,
and skipped myself into feeling good,
I jump around and then once more
I skip back home,
        to my front door.

31

Cat's Cradle Tie-Up

Left finger moves right
        and pulls out the string.
Right finger moves left
        and does the same thing.
Now pinch thumbs and pinkies
        and stretch the string tight
And shift middle fingers —
        it's sure to be right!
Now I turn it to face you,
        I'M GOING TO SNEEZE!!
ATCHOOOOOOOOOOOOOOOOOOOOOO!
Help! Get me out
        of this cat's cradle, PLEASE!

32

Tic Tac Toe

tic tac toe
it's time to go
tic tac head
get out of bed
tic tac finger
don't you linger
tic tac nose
get on your clothes
tic tac leg
don't lay an egg
tic tac thumb
come, shake your bum
tic tac toe
it's time to show
that you'll beat me
at tic tac toe

33

Hide and Seek

1...2...3...4...5...6...7
under a table?
  behind a chair?
    in the broom closet...
    who'd look there?

8...9...10...11
in the basement
  beside the dryer?
    or upstairs
    by the amplifier?

12...13...14...15...16...17...18...19...20
in the old coats?
  behind the skis?
    how about near
    the big deep freeze?

21...22...23...24...25...26...27...28...29...30
where won't they look?
where haven't I tried?
the finding is easy!
  It's SURE hard to hide!

Sun Sun Go Away

Sun sun go away,
      shine again another day.
Rain rain
      come and stay,
So you and I can go and play.

In my rain boots, slicker, hat
I'll go splish and splittery-splat,
I'll go puddle-jumping — PLOP!
I'll go muddy-thumping — SLOP!
I'll sing your song of dripping drops.
I'll dance your dance of flippy-flops.

I'll be your friend,
      drop down my way!
It's with you I want to play.
Rain,
      I want to play with YOU!
You see my rain gear's all brand new!

36

Mud-Puddle Tug-O-War

We'll find a muddy spot to play.
    We'll yank and tug and heave away.
You'll pull this way —
                we'll jerk that
till one side falls —
        FLIPPERY-FLAT!!
As mud spurts way up in the air
and splotches us from shoe to hair,
We'll give a cheer — YES!!! — then we'll roar —
"Hooray for mud-puddle tug-o-war!"

Cloud Watch

Now...
      a tortoise is racing
                a hare,
    a lion is chasing
                a mouse,
    a hippo -- a snail,
    a poodle -- a whale,
    a seal is embracing a house.

Now...
    the tortoise -- it
        flipped past the hare,
  the lion and mouse
        whipped away!
        and...
            hippo, snail,
    poodle and whale,
    all slipped in
        the cloud house
           to play!

Losing My Marbles

I lost my marbles
       in a game of keepsies,
       my cat's eyes,
       my clearies,
I lost heapsees,
       my corkscrews,
       bumboozers,
       my milkie peewees,
       my puries,
       my glassies,
       my shiny steelies
without my marbles,
       I know I'm through
       I can't imagine what
       I can do.
Without my marbles,
       I'm stuck at home
And that's why I'm writing
       this lost marble poem.

39

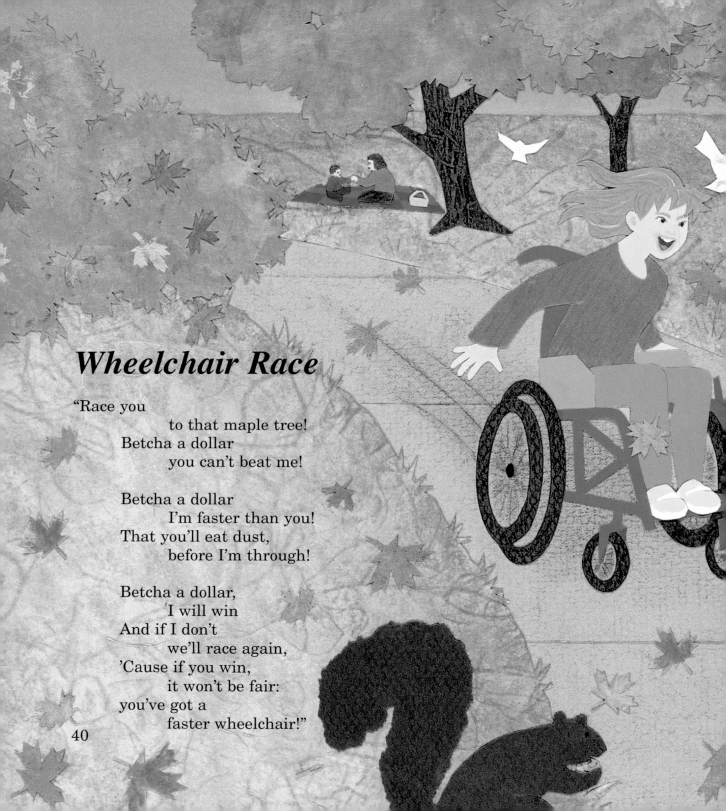

Wheelchair Race

"Race you
　　　　　to that maple tree!
Betcha a dollar
　　　　　you can't beat me!

Betcha a dollar
　　　　　I'm faster than you!
That you'll eat dust,
　　　　　before I'm through!

Betcha a dollar,
　　　　　I will win
And if I don't
　　　　　we'll race again,
'Cause if you win,
　　　　　it won't be fair:
you've got a
　　　　　faster wheelchair!"

40

41

HOPSCOTCH

Hopscotch
1   2
3
happily   I
hopping
roam

Hopscotch
7   8
9
I   hold the
stone
and   hop
for
home

42

WHEELBARROW RIDE

I bump up and down
    like a sack of potatoes.
I roll all around
    like a crop of tomatoes.

I jerk to the front
      to the back
      and the side

when Mom gives me
    a wheelbarrow ride!

43

Let's Play Tag!

"Tunnel!
      crawl through those legs!"
"Honking Goose!
      go sit on eggs"
"Hospital!"
  "Candle!
      melt and sag"

"There's a million ways —
      so let's play
          TAG!"

"You're IT!!!!"   "You're IT!!!!"
"You're IT!!!!"   "You're IT!!!!"

"I'M   IT!!!"

44

FOLLOW THE LEADER

Follow the leader! Follow me!

Hands on your knees
　　wiggle your hips
　　now spin in spirals
　　and smack your lips

Hop by this tree
　　and give it a hug
　　flap your hands 'round
　　and buzz like a bug

Follow the leader! Follow me!

Run past the garbage
　　smell a flower
　　now mess up your hair
　　you're taking a shower

Under the slide
　　over the swings
　　parade all around
　　like queens and kings

stop cold and freeze
　　now I'll follow you
　　who else wants to lead?
　　let's choose someone new!

Rollerblading Blues

yikes and yeeks,
these things are fast —
       they slip before I'm standing

one shoots left
one shoots right
       I do a bum-crash landing!

I wear a helmet,
       pads for my knees
       and straps to guard my wrists

But they don't help my bum at all —
       I fall
       in turny twists

And since I'm not an armored knight
       or a bony armadillo
Next time, I'm wrapping
       'round my bum
       a big, fat foamy pillow.

Caterpillar Sleep
& Butterfly Morning

I'll roll up in my blanket,
    wind it 'round me tight.
      I'll hide me from the starlight,
        just tonight.

I'll turn my face
    from the wide-eyed moon.
      I'll fall asleep in my warm cocoon.

I'll wake up in the morning,
    when the sun's up high!
    And tomorrow I'll be . . .
      a playful butterfly.

48